A Note to Parents

Welcome to REAL KIDS READERS, a series of phonics-based books for children who are beginning to read. In the classroom, educators use phonics to teach children how to sound out unfamiliar words, providing a firm foundation for reading skills. At home, you can use REAL KIDS READERS to reinforce and build on that foundation, because the books follow the same basic phonic guidelines that children learn in school.

Of course the best way to help your child become a good reader is to make the experience fun—and REAL KIDS READERS do that, too. With their realistic story lines and lively characters, the books engage children's imaginations. With their clean design and sparkling photographs, they provide picture clues that help new readers decipher the text. The combination is sure to entertain young children and make them truly want to read.

REAL KIDS READERS have been developed at three distinct levels to make it easy for children to read at their own pace.

- LEVEL 1 is for children who are just beginning to read.
- LEVEL 2 is for children who can read with help.
- LEVEL 3 is for children who can read on their own.

A controlled vocabulary provides the framework at each level. Repetition, rhyme, and humor help increase word skills. Because children can understand the words and follow the stories, they quickly develop confidence. They go back to each book again and again, increasing their proficiency and sense of accomplishment, until they're ready to move on to the next level. The result is a rich and rewarding experience that will help them develop a lifelong love of reading.

To Charles Tidd for his support,
and to Jessica and Bryan Tidd for their inspiration
—L. V. T.

Special thanks to Lands' End, Dodgeville, WI, for providing clothing.

Produced by DWAI / Seventeenth Street Productions, Inc.
Reading Specialist: Virginia Grant Clammer

Library of Congress Cataloging-in-Publication Data

Tidd, Louise Vitellaro.
  Lost and found / Louise Vitellaro Tidd ; photographs by Dorothy Handelman.
      p.   cm. — (Real kids readers. Level 2)
  Summary: Nate's search for his missing sneaker leads him to many other things
he has lost and is delighted to find again.
  ISBN 0-7613-2020-2 (lib. bdg.). — ISBN 0-7613-2045-8 (pbk.)
  [1. Lost and found possessions—Fiction.] I. Handelman, Dorothy, ill.
II. Title. III. Series.
PZ7.T4245Lo 1998
[E]—dc21   98-5575
                                                                     CIP
                                                                     AC

pbk: 10 9 8 7 6 5 4 3 2 1
lib: 10 9 8 7 6 5 4 3 2 1

Lost and Found

By Louise Vitellaro Tidd

Photographs by Dorothy Handelman

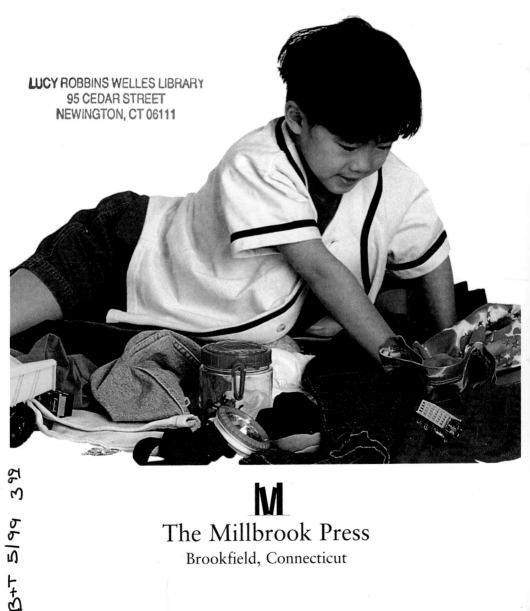

M
The Millbrook Press
Brookfield, Connecticut

It is a warm, sunny day.
Nate wants to play outside.
But he can only find one sneaker.
Where could his other sneaker be?

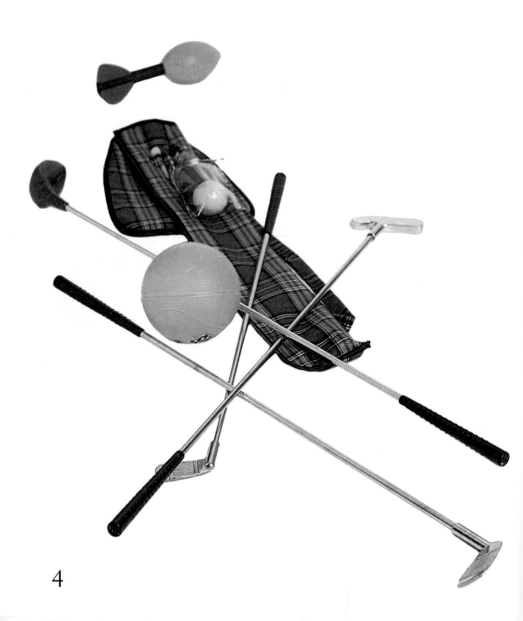

Maybe his big sister, Kim, has seen it.
"I want to go outside," Nate says.
"But I can't find my other sneaker.
Do you know where it is?"

Kim rolls her eyes.
"You can never find your stuff,"
she says.
"I don't know where
your dumb sneaker is.
Maybe it's under your bed."

Nate thinks Kim could be right.
He goes to his room.
He looks under his bed.

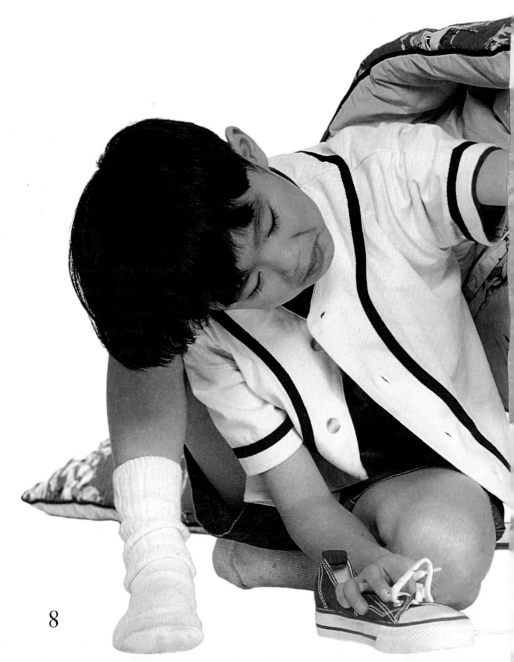

The lost sneaker is not there.
But Nate does find something else!

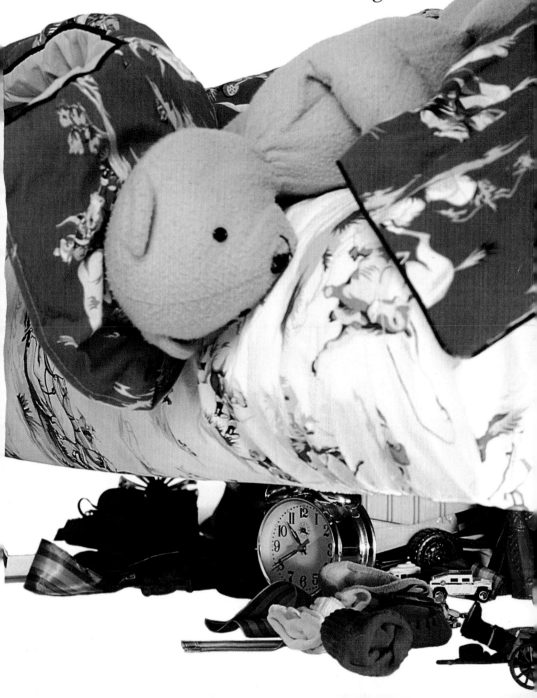

"My dump truck!" says Nate.
"So that's where I left it."
Nate is happy to find his truck.
But he still wants his sneaker.
Where else can he look for it?

Maybe the sneaker is in his closet.
Nate opens the door.
He looks under a pile of pants.
The lost sneaker is not there.
But he does find something else!

It is a joke book he thought was lost.
Nate reads a joke:
"Why did the boy walk over the hill?
Because he could not walk under it."
Nate grins.
"That's a good one," he says.
But he still needs his sneaker.
Nate's sneaker is not under his bed.
It is not in his closet.
Where could it be?

Maybe it is under the big chair.
"Lift your feet," Nate says to Kim.
He looks under the chair.
The lost sneaker is not there.
But he does find something else!

It is a robot he played with last week.
He starts it up.
The robot beeps and walks.
"Cool!" says Nate.
But he still has not found his sneaker.

It is not under his bed.
It is not in his closet.
It is not under the big chair.
Where could it be?

Maybe Nate's dog, King, took it.
Nate looks under King's bed.
The lost sneaker is not there.
But he does find something else!

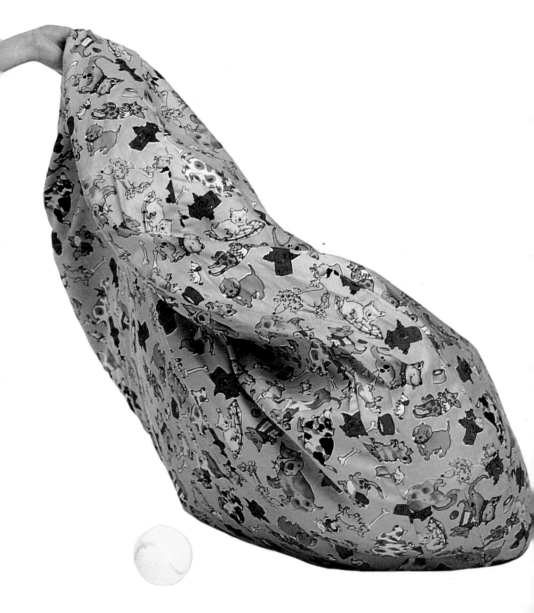

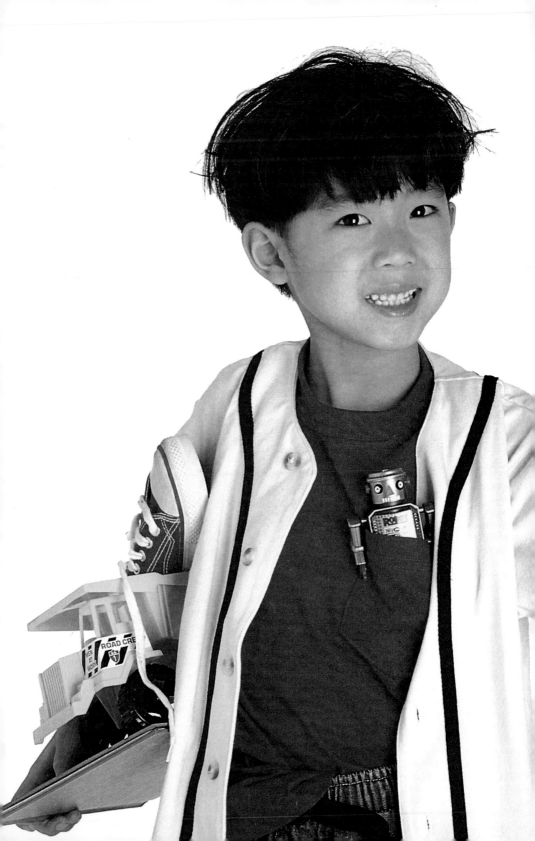

"So this is where King hid my ball,"
says Nate.
He will play ball with King later.
But now he wants to find his sneaker.
"My sneaker is not under my bed,"
says Nate.
"It is not in my closet
or under the chair.
It is not under King's bed.
So where can it be?"

"Maybe it's in my toy box," says Nate.
"That's a good place to put stuff."

He opens up the box.
He dumps out all the toys.
His lost sneaker is not in the box.
But he does find something else!

"I forgot I had these," says Nate.
He is glad that the blocks are found.
But his sneaker is still lost.
It is not under his bed
or in his closet
or under the chair
or under King's bed
or in the toy box.
Where could it be?

Just then Nate hears Kim call.
"Nate!" she yells. "I just tripped
over your dumb sneaker in the hall.
Come and get it.
Then you can go out and play."

Nate smiles.
"Thanks for finding it," he says.
"But I changed my mind.
Why should I go out?
I have all this great stuff to play with—
right here!"

Phonic Guidelines

Use the following guidelines to help your child read the words in *Lost and Found*.

Short Vowels

When two consonants surround a vowel, the sound of the vowel is usually short. This means you pronounce *a* as in apple, *e* as in egg, *i* as in igloo, *o* as in octopus, and *u* as in umbrella. Short-vowel words in this story include: *bed, big, box, but, can, did, dog, get, had, has, hid, his, Kim, not, put.*

Short-Vowel Words with Consonant Blends

When two or more different consonants are side by side, they usually blend to make a combined sound. In this story, short-vowel words with consonant blends include: *blocks, dump, glad, grins, just, King, last, left, lift, lost, pants, stuff, truck.*

Double Consonants

When two identical consonants appear side by side, one of them is silent. In this story, double-consonants appear in the short-vowel words *hill, still, will, yells,* and in the *all*-family words *all, ball, call, hall.*

R-Controlled Vowels

When a vowel is followed by the letter *r*, its sound is changed by the *r*. In this story, words with *r*-controlled vowels include: *are, for, her, starts.*

Long Vowel and Silent E

If a word has a vowel and ends with an *e*, usually the vowel is long and the *e* is silent. Long vowels are pronounced the same way as their alphabet names. In this story, words with a long vowel and silent *e* include: *joke, Nate, pile, place, smiles.*

Double Vowels

When two vowels are side by side, usually the first vowel is long and the second vowel is silent. Double-vowel words in this story include: *beeps, day, hears, needs, play, reads, seen, sneaker, week.*

Diphthongs

Sometimes when two vowels (or a vowel and a consonant) are side by side, they combine to make a diphthong—a sound that is different from long or short vowel sounds. Diphthongs are: *au/aw, ew, oi/oy, ou/ow.* In this story, words with diphthongs include: *boy, found, now, out, toy.*

Consonant Digraphs

Sometimes when two different consonants are side by side, they make a digraph that represents a single new sound. Consonant digraphs are: *ch, sh, th, wh.* In this story, words with digraphs include: *chair, changed, thanks, that, then, there, these, thinks, this, where, why, with.*

Silent Consonants

Sometimes when two different consonants appear side by side, one of them is silent. In this story, words with silent consonants include: *dumb, know, walk.*

Sight Words

Sight words are those words that a reader must learn to recognize immediately—by sight— instead of by sounding them out. They occur with high frequency in easy texts. Sight words not included in the above categories are: *a, be, because, book, come, could, do, does, else, find, go, goes, good, he, here, I, is, it, look, maybe, my, one, only, opens, other, over, says, she, should, sister, to, under, up, wants, was, you, your.*